BAKUGAN

GAMING GUIDE

SCHOLASTIC INC.

All rights reserved. Published by Scholastic Inc., *Publishers since 1920.* SCHOLASTIC and associated logos are trademarks and/or registered trademarks of Scholastic Inc.

The publisher does not have any control over and does not assume any responsibility for author or third-party websites or their content.

This book is a work of fiction. Names, characters, places, and incidents are either the product of the author's imagination or are used fictitiously, and any resemblance to actual persons, living or dead, business establishments, events, or locales is entirely coincidental.

ISBN 978-1-338-57491-3

10 9 8 7 6 5 4 3 2 1   19 20 21 22 23

Printed in the U.S.A.   40
First printing 2019

Designed by Cheung Tai
Book design by Jeff Shake

TABLE OF CONTENTS

WHAT IS BAKUGAN: BATTLE PLANET?

WELCOME BRAWLERS!

This guide will tell you everything you need to know about the Brawling games you can play as part of *Bakugan: Battle Planet*.

Bakugan: Battle Planet is an animated TV series about creatures known as Bakugan and the Brawlers that discover and befriend them.

The Bakugan Battling Game lets you experience what it's like to be a Brawler and unleash your Bakugan against opponents.

To win the game, you'll need to outroll and overpower your opponent. Let's get Brawling!

There are two awesome ways to play
the Bakugan Brawling Game.

TOY BATTLING GAME

In the Toy Battling Game, you and your Bakugan will
face off against another team on the Hide Matrix!
The B Power of your Bakugan and BakuCores will
determine the winner of each Brawl.

TRADING CARD GAME

Once you've mastered the Toy Battling Game, the Trading Card Game adds even more fun and strategy with collectible cards, special abilities, heroes, and evolutions.

Pact of Darkness — ◇ 4
Flip.
○ non-⊖
Sacrifice - You may discard a card to play this for free.

Titan Howlkor Ultra — ⚡ 5
◼1300 | Evo | 5 ⬆
⬆: +5⬆

Stole Shot — ⬥ 2
Action
Draw a card.
Domination - If your Bakugan hold the most BakuCores, draw two cards instead.

Titan Dragonoid — ◇ 6
◼1200 | Evo | 6 ⬆

Hyper Mantonoid Ultra — ◇ 4
◼1000 | Evo | 1 ⬆
This gets +1⬆ for each Energy card you have in play.

Deafening Roar — ◇ 3
Action
-600◼

Furious Blast — ◇ 3
Action
+6⬆
Fury: If you have no cards in hand, return this to your hand.

Magnus — ◇ 8
Hero
When you play this, a Bakugan gets +5000◼.
Victor: You may discard a card to give a Bakugan +⬆ equal to the discarded card's Energy cost.

Lia Venegas — ◇ 10
Hero
When you play this, search your deck for a Hero card and reveal it, then put it into your hand. Shuffle your deck.
+10⬆ to your attacks, if you control five or more Hero cards in play.

Hyper Trox — ◇ 3
◼900 | 2 ⬆
When you play this, choose a player to discard a card.

Hyper Dragonoid — ⚡ 1
◼600 | Evo | 8 ⬆

Olivia Styles — ◇ 6
Hero
Non-⊖ Bakugan get -300◼.

Light as a Feather — ⬥ 8
Flip
Put this into your hand and draw a card.

Hyperdrive — ◇ 3
Flip
Both players may Energize the top two cards of their deck.

Counter Outsiders — ◇ 3
Flip
○ non-⊖

Lava Flow — ◇ 0
Flip
+1⬆

Hyper Maxotaur Ultra — ◇ 4
◼900 | Evo | 4 ⬆
⬆: +10⬆

Rite of Darkus — ◇ 5
Action
Choose a player to discard a card for each ⊖ Bakugan on your team.

Hurricane Slash — ◇ 3
Action
+200◼
Flow - If you played another card this turn, return this to your hand.

Dan Kouzo — ◇ 4
Hero
When you open a Bakugan, reveal the top card of your deck. If it is not a Flip card, you may play it for free.

Strata — ◇ 2
Hero
All players draw an additional card each turn.

HOW TO PLAY BAKUGAN: TOY BATTLING GAME

WHAT YOU NEED FOR THE TOY BATTLING GAME

To play the Toy Battling Game, you'll need six BakuCores, three Bakugan, and their matching Character cards.

The Bakucore types should match the ones on your Character cards. Your Character cards will also tell you the B Power, Damage Rating, and if your Bakugan has any special abilities.

Set your Bakugan in the closed position on their matching Character cards, face down.

You will use your BakuCores to build your Hide Matrix in the middle of the playing area.

Trox Ultra

B300

1

Victor - You may energize a card in your hand uncharged.

Dragonoid

B200

5

To set up your game, each player will need six BakuCores. BakuCores are metal, hexagonal tiles that cause your Bakugan to open and give your Bakugan certain powers when picked up. There are five different types of BakuCores, shown by the icon on the back of the tile:

 Helix

Fist

Shield

Flaming Fist

Magic Shield

The six BakuCores that you play with must match the symbols on your team's Character cards.

EXAMPLE:

Garganoid Ultra

B300

5

Hydorous

B200

6

+400 B

⊙:+6

The front of the tile shows the effect each BakuCore has. For example, a BakuCore might increase or decrease your Bakugan's B Power when picked up.

THE HIDE MATRIX

First, flip a BakuCore to determine who will go first. Then players take turns placing each BakuCore face down in the center of the playing area. This will create your Hide Matrix!

The Hide Matrix is where all your Brawls will go down, so this part is important!

You can place your BakuCores wherever you want—the only rule is that each BakuCore must touch one entire side to another BakuCore.

A less-powerful Bakugan can win a Brawl if it lands on the right BakuCore, so be strategic in where you place yours.

ROLLING YOUR BAKUGAN

Each player chooses an unopened Bakugan to roll this turn. Roll your Bakugan toward the Hide Matrix at the same time. Try to release at least two card lengths away from the nearest BakuCore.

Each Bakugan has a little arrow showing the ideal direction to roll, but you can roll however you want! Your goal is for your Bakugan to land on one of the BakuCores and open.

When your Bakugan rolls over a BakuCore, it might flip open! It also might grab on to the BakuCore and not let go.

Which Bakugan you choose, which BakuCore you pick up, and even the Bakugan crashing together on the Hide Matrix can all affect the outcome.

BRAWLING

If only one Bakugan opens, that player wins the Brawl.

If neither Bakugan opens, both players roll again.

If both open, it's time to Brawl!

Flip over the Character cards for the open Bakugan. Add the B Power on the Bakugan's Character card to any B Power boosts on the BakuCores. The player with the highest total B Power wins!

If the B Power is a tie, the Bakugan with the highest Attack Damage wins! If that is also a tie, both players close their Bakugan and roll again.

The winner of the Brawl places their open Bakugan back on its Character card, still holding its BakuCore. The other player closes their Bakugan and places it back on its Character card to be rerolled. That player's BakuCore goes back on the Hide Matrix.

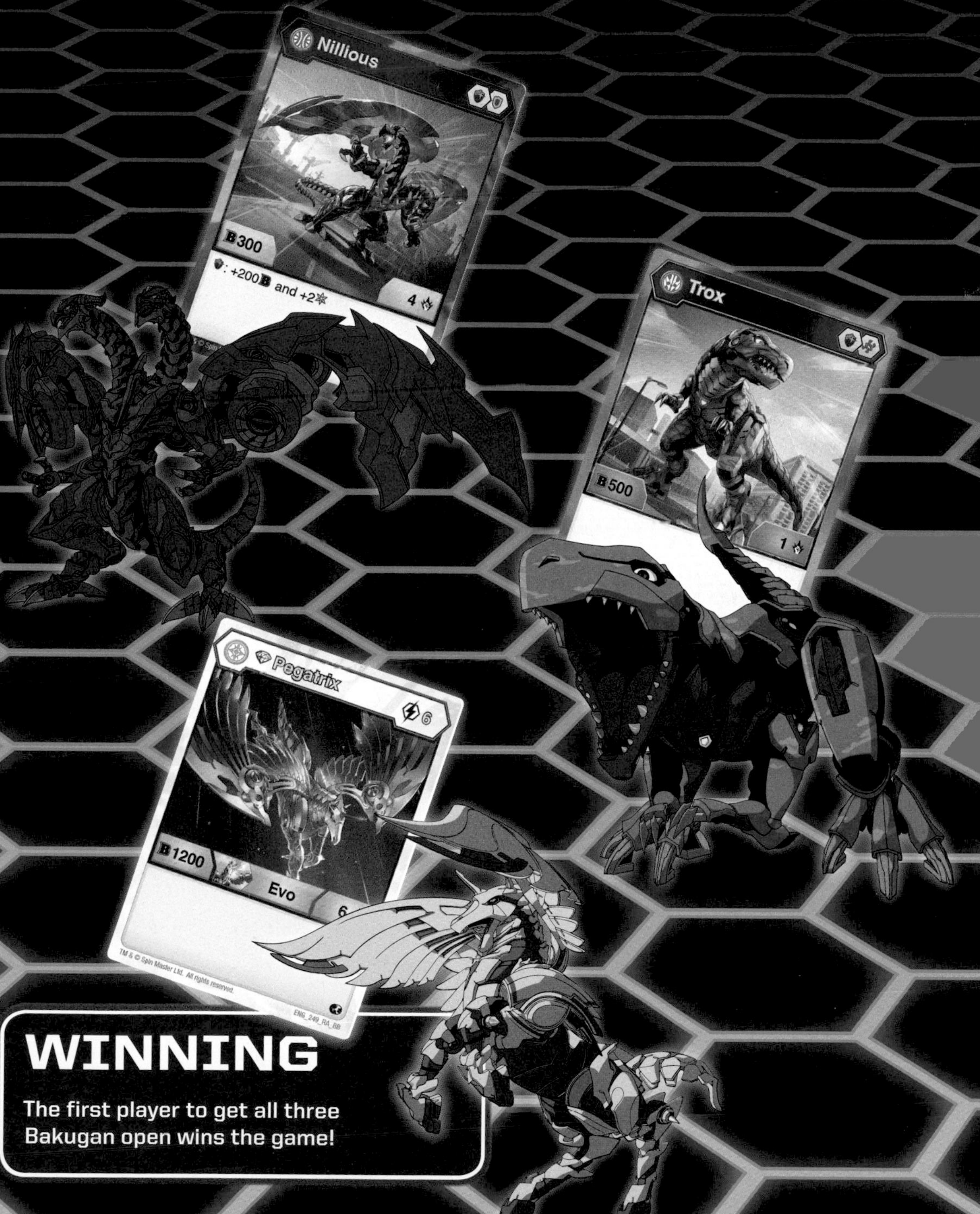

Nillious
300
: +200 and +2
4
Trox
500
1
Pegatrix
6
1200
Evo
6
TM & © Spin Master Ltd. All rights reserved.
ENG_249_RA_BB

WINNING

The first player to get all three Bakugan open wins the game!

HOW TO PLAY BAKUGAN: TRADING CARD GAME

WHAT YOU NEED FOR THE TRADING CARD GAME

Now that you've mastered the Toy Battling Game, why not try the Trading Card Game? It has all the awesome brawling action of the Toy Battling Game, with even more strategies, characters, and surprises.

Your deck will be filled with cards that match the Factions of your chosen Bakugan—so it's even more important to choose carefully.

Titan Howlkor Ultra ⚡ 5

B 1000   EVO   1 ⚔

This has +1 🔥 for each Flip card in your discard pile.

ENG_245_AR_BB

To play the Bakugan Trading Card Game, each player needs:

- Three Bakugan and their matching Character cards

- Six BakuCores

- A 40-card deck

Your deck will be filled with cards that match the Factions of your chosen Bakugan—so it's even more important to choose carefully. Turn the page to learn all about what the different Factions offer.

CHOOSE YOUR FACTIONS

There are six Factions to choose from, and they all use different strategies to win each battle and game. You will build your deck with cards that match the Factions of your chosen Bakugan.

DARKUS

Darkus is the Faction of power and greed. A Darkus player is willing to sacrifice anything for victory! Master manipulators, Darkus players can strategically weaken their opponent up until the moment they strike.

AQUOS

Aquos, the Faction of focus and precision, is constantly searching for the perfect moment to strike. Aquos is weakest against decks that force them to use their cards before the ideal moment.

HAOS

Haos is the Faction of momentum and control. A Haos player wants to gain strategic advantages and maintain leads by holding the most BakuCores. Haos is weakest against chaotic, unpredictable strategies.

PYRUS

Pyrus is the Faction of aggression. A Pyrus player will strike first and ask questions later! Pyrus wants to attack and win quickly through burst damage and a mighty DoubleStrike attack!

VENTUS

Ventus is the Faction of natural growth and decay. It harnesses the power of nature to increase its Energy. Believing "you grow, or you die," Ventus players try to grow quickly! They're known to defend themselves by reducing their opponent's ability to attack.

AURELUS

For a time, this powerful Faction was mysterious, only showing up in Bakugan and their Evolutions. That all changes with Age of Aurelus . . .

TYPES OF CARDS

CHARACTER CARDS

are placed under your Bakugan on the playing field. They tell you everything you need to know about the Bakugan you are brawling with.

Mantonoid

B 500

2

Turtonium Ultra

B 500

3

Dragonoid

B 200

5

CHARACTER CARDS HAVE BLACK CARD BACKS!

ABILITY CARDS
are what make up
your deck. There
are four types of
Ability cards:

ACTION

Darkus Strike
⚡ 3

◎ Action

+6⚡. If ◎, choose a player to discard
a card.

HERO

Dan Kouzo
⚡ 4

Hero

When you open a Bakugan, reveal
the top card of your deck. If its not a
Flip card, you may play it for free.

EVO

Maxotaur Ultra
⚡ 10

B 1500   Evo   15⚡

FLIP

Cease Ventus
⚡ 0

◎ Flip

ABILITY CARDS HAVE RED CARD BACKS!

23

CHARACTER CARDS

Each Bakugan has a Character card that tells you everything you need to know about your Bakugan and how to battle with it.

This symbol tells you which Faction your Bakugan comes from. This Fangzor is from the Aurelus Faction.

This is the name of your Bakugan.

This tells you which types of BakuCores to use with your Bakugan. If you want to use this Aurelus Fangzor in battle, choose any two Shield BakuCores to place in the Hide Matrix.

Fangzor

B 700

2

This is your Bakugan's **B** power. **B** power determines which Bakugan triumphs in each Brawl!

This is your Bakugan's Damage Rating. If your Bakugan wins its brawl, this is how much damage it does to your opponent.

: +5

ENG_299_CC_BB

This section of the card will tell you if your Bakugan has any special abilities. This Aurelus Fangzor deals five extra damage if it wins a Brawl by landing on a Shield Bakucore.

Your deck will be full of Ability cards. They each do something different.

This is the name of the action or character you're playing.

This tells you how much Energy it will cost you to play this card—make sure you have enough Energy when you need it!

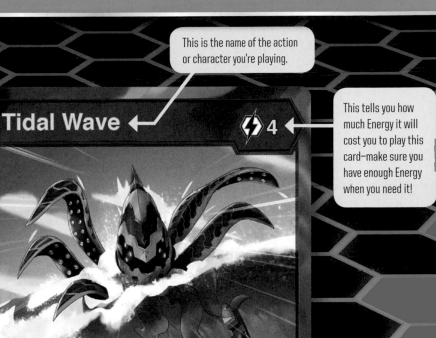

Tidal Wave

⚡ 4

● Action

+7 🔥

TM & © Spin Master Ltd. All rights reserved.

ENG_23_CO_BB

This tells you which Faction this card comes from. Your deck will be full of cards from the same Factions as your Bakugan.

This tells you what type of card this is.

This section tells you what special abilities the Tidal Wave card has. If you play this card after winning a Brawl, you can deal an extra seven damage to your opponent!

TURN THE PAGE TO FIND OUT MORE ABOUT EACH TYPE OF ABILITY CARD!

ABILITY CARDS

You can play an Action card from your hand at any time except during the Damage Phase (more about the different phases later). Action cards might have an effect on B Power, Attack Damage, your own hand or deck, and more. Learn more about the different kinds of actions in the Advanced Deck Building section!

Action name

Energy cost

Cycling Warmth ⚡2

Faction

This section describes the action. If you play this card after winning a Brawl, you can deal an extra two damage to your opponent, then return it to the bottom of your deck—that increases your life total!

Action cards will always say "Action" here

Action

+2⚡, then return this to the bottom of your deck.

ENG_85_CO_BB

A Hero card, when played, stays on the board and continues to have an effect on the game until it is removed. Place any played Hero card faceup next to your deck.

Hero name

Col. Armstrong Tripp ⚡3

Energy cost

Faction

Hero

Hero cards will always say "Hero" here

When one of your Bakugan attacks, draw a card.

ENG_200_RA_BB

This section describes the Hero's special abilities. If you've played Lightning, he stays on the board and causes your Flip cards to cost one less Energy for the rest of the game—unless your opponent finds a way to remove him!

EVO CARDS

Evo cards are how you level up your Bakugan! Play one from your hand by placing it on top of the Character card for the Bakugan you are evolving. After that, your Bakugan has new, higher stats!

Your deck should have Evo cards that match both the names and Factions of your starting Bakugan.

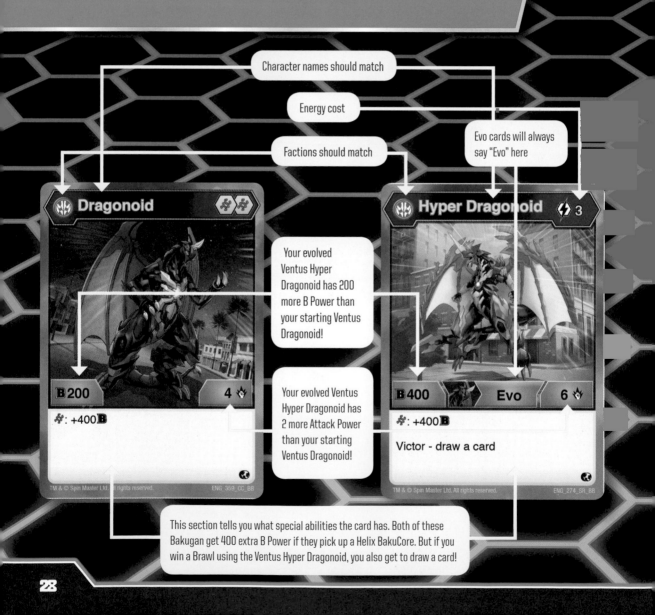

Character names should match

Energy cost

Factions should match

Evo cards will always say "Evo" here

Dragonoid

Hyper Dragonoid ⚡3

Your evolved Ventus Hyper Dragonoid has 200 more B Power than your starting Ventus Dragonoid!

B 200   4

B 400   Evo   6

⚔: +400 B

⚔: +400 B

Victor - draw a card

Your evolved Ventus Hyper Dragonoid has 2 more Attack Power than your starting Ventus Dragonoid!

This section tells you what special abilities the card has. Both of these Bakugan get 400 extra B Power if they pick up a Helix BakuCore. But if you win a Brawl using the Ventus Hyper Dragonoid, you also get to draw a card!

Flip cards are not played from your hand—they can only be played directly from the deck during the Damage Phase. Sometimes they stop damage, and sometimes they simply give you a chance to get a benefit from losing a Brawl.

Ability name

Energy cost

Halt Darkus

Faction

Flip

Flip cards will always say "Flip" here

This section describes the Flip card's special abilities. If you flip this card over while taking damage from a Darkus Bakugan, the damage will stop!

Flip cards are oriented differently than all other types of cards.

ENG_156_CO_BB

FLIP CARDS

BUILDING YOUR DECK

THE BASICS

Here are the most important things that all decks have in common:

- 40 cards

- Action, Hero, Evo, or Flip cards—usually a mix of all four!

- The Factions of the cards match the Factions of the brawling Bakugan

- Any Evo cards in the deck match the Faction *and* name of at least one of your brawling Bakugan

- No more than three copies of any one card

After that, you can build your deck however you like! Try different combos and strategies—have fun with it!

Hero's Demise ◊4

Lava Boost ◊6

Shuryuken ◊2

Action

+1. Return this to your hand.

Ventus Moonbeam ◊3

Action

-4

Turbo: If you have the most Energy cards in play, -8 instead.

Blinding Glam ⚡3

Action

-3 to an enemy Bakugan or +3 to one of your Bakugan.

E | ⚡5

BEE | ⚡1

Hero

When you select a Bakugan to roll, you may turn a BakuCore on the field face up.

Wynton Styles | ⚡4

...ou open a Bakugan, +3...
...rn.

Hero

When you open a Bakugan, you may Energize the top card of your deck.

If you have 15 or more Energy cards in play, your Bakugan have +1500 **B**...

...nation - If your Bakugan...
...g the most BakuCores,...
...r attacks.

China Riot | ⚡4

Hero

+1⚡ to your attacks.

If this is discarded, you may play it for free.

Pyrus Dominance | ⚡5

Flip

...destroy an Energy card.

Repel Outsiders | ⚡3

Flip

Fading Dash | ⚡1

Flip

Retract one of your Bakugan that didn't open this turn. If you do, draw two cards.

Cease Outsiders | ⚡3

Flip

⚡ non-⊖

Haos Ascendancy | ⚡5

Flip

⚡ non-⊖, then put this into your hand.

Titan Trox | ⚡5

Hyper Dragonoid | ⚡4

Titan Fangzor | ⚡5

B800 | Evo | 3 ⚡

⚡: +2⚡ and 𝔅

Evo

...ou may Energize the ...our deck uncharged.

Hyper Pegatrix | ⚡3

B1100 | Evo | 6 ⚡

⚡: +500 **B**

Titan Pegatrix | ⚡4

B1000 | Evo | 4 ⚡

⚡: +500 **B** and +5⚡

SETTING UP THE TRADING CARD GAME

Place your three Bakugan on their facedown Character cards. Flip a BakuCore to see who goes first, then take turns placing your BakuCores. Don't forget your BakuCores should match the symbols on your Bakugan's Character cards!

You'll also need places to put your deck, a discard pile, your Energy cards, and any Hero cards you might play.

DRAW PHASE

Once you have your Hide Matrix set up, each player draws five cards from the top of their deck at the same time. Now the game begins!

YOUR DECK AND LIFE TOTAL

In the Bakugan Trading Card Game, your deck is your life total—each player tries to do damage to the other by causing them to put cards from their deck directly into their discard pile. The first player to run out of cards in the Damage Phase loses!

This means that anytime you can use Ability cards to return cards to your deck, you are increasing your life total and chances to win.

The deck is also where you get the cards for your hand. Most cards can only be played from your hand, not your discard pile.

So keep an eye on that deck!

Hyper Hydorous 3

Evo

B800

4

When you play an Action on this, it gets +2.

Hero
Your Bakugan have +1.

Halt Darkus

Flip

Cyndeus Stand

Action
Shuffle any number of your hand into you each card shuffled

Cutepocalypse 4

Action
+500 B
Domination - If yo most BakuCores,

ENERGY PHASE

After the Draw Phase for each turn comes the Energy Phase. This is your chance to add a card to your Energy Zone.

Energy is the cost you pay to play Action, Evo, and Hero cards from your hand—or Flip cards during the Damage Phase.

During the Energy Phase, each player may choose one Ability card to Energize by placing it facedown in the Energy Zone as Energy. Energy gives you the ability to play other cards, but be careful—once a card has been Energized, it can't be picked back up and used as an Ability card.

Tip: Flip cards make great Energy cards—you can't play them from your hand, so once you've drawn them, Energy is a good way to use them.

Used Energy cards are turned on their sides and cannot be used again this turn. They're now considered uncharged. At the end of each turn, both players charge their Energy cards back up by turning them upright again. Then they can be used again next turn.

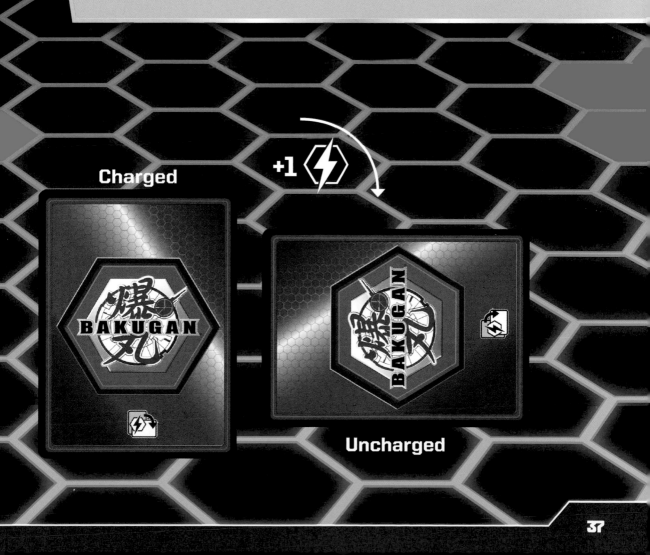

Charged

+1

Uncharged

PLAYING CARDS

During the Energy Phase, Brawl, Victory, and End phases, players may use Energy to play Action, Evo, and Hero cards.

Pay the Energy cost by uncharging your Energy cards—turn your Energy cards sideways and place down the card you want to play. For example, if your Ability card costs 3 Energy, turn 3 Energy Cards sideways.

After the action of the card has been taken, place the Ability card In the discard pile unless it says otherwise.

This is a good time to play cards that might help you win your next Brawl—because it's coming up next!

Flooding Waters ⚡1

Action

+200**B** for each ⬡ Bakugan on your team.

TM & © Spin Master Ltd. All rights reserved.   ENG_9_RA_BB

This card costs 1 Energy

To play it, uncharge one Energy card by turning it sideways

BRAWLING

After the Energy Phase, it's time to roll!

Each player chooses an unopened Bakugan they will roll this turn. Players roll their Bakugan toward the Hide Matrix at the same time, releasing at least two card lengths away from the nearest BakuCore.

If no Bakugan opens, roll again.

If only one Bakugan opens, that player turns over their Character card and is the Victor!

If both players' Bakugan open, they both turn over their Character cards.

Combine the B score from each Character card with the B score from any BakuCores that were picked up.

×300 B

TM & © Spin Master Ltd. All rights reserved.

Players may play cards to modify their B Power or anything else—if they have the Energy to spend!

Keep playing cards until both players pass—remember, if your opponent still has charged Energy, they might still play cards!

Brawling in the Trading Card Game is similar to the Toy Battling Game (see p. 16), except for what happens if there is a tie. In the Trading Card Game, ties are settled by each player flipping over a card from their deck. The player with the higher Energy cost on their card wins the Brawl.

TIP: The arrow on your Bakugan notes the roll direction for best performance.

VICTORY PHASE

The player with the highest B Power wins the Brawl and is the Victor!

Now it is time for the Victory Phase.

The winner of the Brawl sets their open Bakugan on its Character card.

The other player returns their Bakugan to ball form, places it on its Character card, and returns any BakuCores it picked up to the Hide Matrix.

Each player may play cards to modify attack until both players pass. Maybe the Victor has cards that increase Attack Damage, or maybe the other player has cards that reduce Attack Damage.

DAMAGE PHASE

The Victor combines the Attack Damage from the Character card, any cards played, and any BakuCores it picked up.

The Victor deals damage to the opponent for each Attack Damage it has. The opponent flips one card into their discard pile from the top of their deck for each damage they are dealt.

If a Flip card is exposed while flipping, the damaged player may pay the Energy cost of that Flip card to play it if applicable. Flip cards will note which Factions can and cannot be countered.

If a Flip card is played, it must be used right away, before any more cards are flipped.

Counter Aquos ⚡0
Flip

Shadow Breath ⚡4
Flip
Take control of a Hero.
ENG_154_SR_BB

Punish ⚡2
Flip
Choose a player to discard a card.

Counter Pyrus ⚡0
Flip
ENG_143_CO_BB

Blackhole ⚡3
Flip
End the turn. Nothing else can happen this turn, start the next turn. (Cards cannot be played, remaining damage vanishes and Energy Cards do not recharge.)
ENG_146_AR_BB

PLAYING FLIP CARDS

TEAM ATTACK!

If a player wins a Brawl and all three of their Bakugan are open, they deliver a devastating Team Attack!

Instead of the usual Damage Phase, the Victor Bakugan combines the Attack Power of each Bakugan on the team and any BakuCores they picked up.

Tip: The third and final Bakugan to win a Brawl for a team is the one dealing the Team Attack Damage. Keep that in mind when thinking about which Flip cards your opponent is most likely to have in their deck!

After a Team Attack, all three Bakugan return to ball form and all their BakuCores go back to the Hide Matrix.

Players may play Action, Evo, or Hero cards before a turn ends. This is a great time to use up any extra Energy you still have charged, because this is your last chance!

Once both players are done playing cards, they recharge their uncharged Energy cards and begin a new Draw Phase. Starting with the second turn, only draw one card per turn during the Draw Phase.

END OF TURN

WINNING THE TRADING CARD GAME

A player who makes their opponent flip a card from their deck when they have no more cards left wins the game!

A player with no cards left in their deck cannot lose during Draw Phase. They can only lose as a result of damage.

ADVANCED DECK BUILDING

READY TO BUILD YOUR ULTIMATE DECK?

In this section, you'll learn all about the different types of Actions, Heroes, Evos, Flips, and strategies each Faction offers and how to use them to build powerful and fun decks to battle with!

CORE ABILITIES AND STRATEGIES

Some types of abilities are available to build into your deck, no matter which Factions you choose. Learning about these is the best way to start digging further into deck building.

ADDING AND SUBTRACTING B POWER AND DAMAGE

How do you win Brawls? With B Power.

How do you win games? With Attack Power.

So one of the simplest, most powerful actions you can take is to increase your own power or decrease your opponent's power.

All Factions have cards of every type that do this.

If your card says + **B**, you can play it to increase your Bakugan's B Power. If it says - **B**, you might play it on your opponent's Bakugan. Either way, you are more likely to win that Brawl.

If your card says - 👊 , you can play it when you lose a Brawl, to take less damage and give yourself more time. If you win a Brawl, playing a card that says + 👊 increases the Attack Damage your opponent takes, getting you closer to winning faster.

DRAW

Your deck is full of awesome cards, and you want to play them. But for most types of cards, you need them to be in your hand first. That's where cards that give you extra Draw come in.

Drawing gets your cards in your hand faster so that you have more options when it comes time to play abilities. It also makes it more likely you'll get a key card into your hand before it hits the discard pile during the Damage Phase.

But be careful—remember, your deck is also your life total. So the more cards in your hand, the faster you need to defeat your opponent before they defeat you! You may even be forced to draw if you want to gain a card's other effects. Draw carefully and don't wait too long to play the cards you draw!

Inspire ⚡1

Action

+1🔥. Draw a card.

ENG_17_CO_BB

RETURNING CARDS TO YOUR DECK OR HAND

You can only play most cards if they're in your hand, and the only cards that count toward your life total are in your deck. But what if you could play a card and still use it again? With some cards, you can.

If the card says "Return this card to your hand," you can put it back in your hand after you play it, giving you the option of playing it again later.

If the card says "Return this card to the bottom of your deck," then you can play the card and then still have it count toward your life total.

Cycling Ichor

⚡5

Action

-8⚡, then return this to the bottom of your deck.

ENG_113_CO_BB

FACTION SYNERGY

Some cards give you extra power if played with certain Factions. If you plan ahead by choosing your Factions and cards carefully, you can make sure you're likely to have the option to take advantage of this kind of synergy.

A card might have a very useful power on its own, but if it says "If ⊛," that means you get something extra if your attacking Bakugan matches the Faction indicated.

Darkus Strike ⚡3

Action

+6⚡. If ⊛, choose a player to discard a card.

ENG_36_CO_BB

EXAMPLE:

Darkus Strike gives you an extra 6 Attack Damage no matter what Faction Bakugan is attacking—awesome! But if that Bakugan happens to be Darkus, you also get to force your opponent to discard!

VICTOR

Either player can play a card during most phases, but some cards have extra abilities if they're played by the Victor of the current Brawl. Check your ability text for the word "Victor"—it may have special instructions that will make you want to save it for a winning Brawl!

Magnus ⚡8

Hero

When you play this, a Bakugan gets +5000.

Victor: You may discard a card to give a Bakugan +✧ equal to the discarded card's Energy cost.

ENG_199_RF_BR

FROSTSTRIKE, SHADOWSTRIKE, AND DOUBLESTRIKE

These are special effects that could show up in more than one—but not all—Factions.

FROSTSTRIKE

When you see this symbol, commonly found on Aquos and Haos cards, Flip cards cost 1 additional Energy for the defending player to play for each point of FrostStrike ✳ the attacking Bakugan has. This makes it harder for the player taking damage to defend themselves from Attack Damage.

Reflection Rays ⚡1

Action

+1 ✳ for each ⊕ Bakugan on your team.

TM & © Spin Master Ltd. All rights reserved.   ENG_72_RA_BB

SHADOWSTRIKE

💲 So far only seen in Darkus, a card with ShadowStrike 💲 gives Bakugan total protection from having their B Power or Attack Damage reduced.

Cloak in Shadow ⚡2

Action

+3⚡ and 💲

ENG_30_CO_BB

DOUBLESTRIKE

🔥 Common on Pyrus cards, DoubleStrike 🔥 doubles the Attack Damage of the Bakugan it's played on.

Molten Helix ⚡4

Action

+2⚡ and 🔥.

ENG_105_CO_BB

WHAT'S NEW IN RESURGENCE

The first big expansion set, Resurgence, introduced awesome new abilities that all the Factions can take advantage of.

WATCH THOSE BAKUCORES

When you're playing with the Resurgence expansion, you're going to want to pay extra attention to which BakuCore your Bakugan is picking up during each Brawl. Many of the new cards give you extra abilities if you pick up a certain BakuCore type.

EXAMPLE: Water to Ice gives your Bakugan an extra 5 Attack Damage. But if your Bakugan has picked up a Shield BakuCore, you also get to draw a card!

Water to Ice ⚡3

Action

+5

If that Bakugan is holding 🛡, draw a card.

ENG_12_CO_BR

REROLLING

When a roll doesn't go the way you want, don't you wish you could try again? Or when your opponent has an amazing roll, don't you wish you could make *them* try again?

With a Reroll Ability card, you might be given the option to roll again. Or you might be forced—or force your opponent!—to roll again.

Spirit Guide ⚡3

◈ Action

+400**B** and you may Reroll your Bakugan.

VERY POWERFUL EVOS

In Resurgence, some of your Evos might have surprisingly powerful special abilities, in addition to amping up that **B** Power and Attack Damage.

Titan Serpenteze Ultra ⚡5

B1000　　Evo　　7 ⚜

When this opens, you may recharge all of your Energy cards.

WHAT'S NEW IN AGE OF AURELUS

The second big expansion, Age of Aurelus, introduces Aurelus Action, Flip, and Hero cards to the mix! But Aurelus isn't the only Faction that gets to play with these new abilities—many have cool effects on all Factions.

AURELUS POWER

This new keyword power gives you big benefits to having at least one Aurelus Bakugan on your team—regardless of what other Factions you might be playing with!

Liqui Darts ⚡3

Action

+400 **B**

Aurelus Power: If you have an Bakugan on your team, this costs 2⚡ less to play.

ENG_6_CO_AA

A COLORFUL TEAM IS A POWERFUL TEAM

Age of Aurelus introduces cards that give you a bonus for playing cards from other Factions. You'll want to mix up your teams and try playing with a multi-Faction deck!

Hyper Vicerox Ultra ⚡2

B700 | Evo | 7 ⬥

When you play a ⊕ or an ⊙ card, this gets +2⬥ this turn.

UNDERDOG BONUSES

We always want our Bakugan to have the most B Power, but sometimes a seemingly less-powerful Bakugan or Evo will offer benefits to starting out behind.

Hyper Cubbo ⚡2

B400 | Evo | 8 ⬥

Underdog: When this opens, if it has lower **B** than the opposing Bakugan, your opponent must discard a card.

AQUOS ABILITIES AND STRATEGIES

If you have an Aquos Bakugan on your team, you can put Aquos cards in your deck. Aquos is all about focus and precision. You control the game by playing the perfect card at the perfect moment.

FLOW

Flow is the exclusive special ability of Aquos. Cards with Flow give you extra abilities if you play them during a turn in which you've already played at least one other card. To take full advantage of your Flow cards, be careful how you spend your Energy and make sure your deck has enough lower-Energy-cost cards so that you have Energy to play multiple cards in a turn.

Ebb ⚡2

Action

+2✳

Flow - If you played another card this turn, +5✳ instead.

ENG_7_CO_BB

NEGATING ACTIONS

The ultimate control ability is to stop your opponent from doing what they want to do. Aquos can do that with cards that negate an action and sometimes even copy it—so that just when your opponent thinks they're going to strike, you strike instead! Knowing the perfect moment to use these cards is key to success—you want to save them for your opponent's most powerful plays, but you don't want to save them until it's too late!

Absorb ⚡4

Action

Negate an Action card. You may copy its effect and make your own selections for it.

ENG_1_AR_BB

RETRACTING BAKUGAN

Similarly, your opponent may think their open Bakugan, that have already won Brawls are safe. But with Aquos in your deck, they can never be sure. You can use cards to force your opponent to retract Bakugan that are already open, putting them that much further away from hitting you with a Team Attack. Other cards may allow you to retract your own Bakugan in exchange for something valuable—like a big B Power boost for a low Energy cost.

Fixation ⚡2

Action

Retract a Bakugan that did not open this turn.

ENG_8_CO_BB

BAKUGAN SYNERGY

Aquos cards are even more powerful when used with Aquos Bakugan. Many cards will give you extra value if used with an Aquos Bakugan—or more than one!

Flooding Waters ⚡1

Action

+200**B** for each ⊕ Bakugan on your team.

ENG_9_RA_BB

WHAT'S NEW FOR AQUOS IN RESURGENCE

SWAPPING BAKUCORES

In addition to the BakuCore-specific actions that all the Factions got in Resurgence, Aquos also gains cards that give you the ability to force Bakugan to *swap* their BakuCores. That gives you even more control over the outcome of Brawls and the perks that may come from holding certain BakuCores. If your opponent picks up the BakuCore you want—or you pick up one you *don't* want—you know what to do!

Aquify ⚡1

Action

Swap the BakuCores attached to the Bakugan you rolled this turn and the opposing Bakugan.

ENG_1_RA_BR

PLAYING CARDS FOR FREE

Resurgence also gives Aquos cards that give you the ability to play certain types of cards for free—so you have an even better chance to activate those Flow cards later on in the turn!

Hurricane Winds ⚡3

Action

+300**B**. You can play an Action card that costs 4⚡ or less for free.

ENG_7_SR_BR

WHAT'S NEW FOR AQUOS IN AGE OF AURELUS

TONS OF DRAW

The new Aquos cards in Age of Aurelus offer some very powerful Draw effects. This will give you plenty of options to trigger your Flow effects without depleting your hand size too much.

Elemental Storm

Action

Aurelus Power: If you have an ⬦ Bakugan on your team, this costs 2⚡ less to play.

Draw five cards.

ENG_4_AR_AA

DARKUS ABILITIES AND STRATEGIES

If you have a Darkus Bakugan on your team, you can put Darkus cards in your deck. Darkus is all about making sacrifices in order to get exactly what you want when you want it. If you play it right, your opponent might even play right into your plans.

SACRIFICE

Sacrifice is the signature move of Darkus, and it is what it sounds like— you give something up in order to get something even better. Sacrifice by discarding a card from your hand. In exchange, depending on the card, you may get a boost that could help you win a Brawl or a game! Flip cards are perfect to discard for Sacrifice, because you can't play them from your hand anyway. But sometimes you may have to give up a card you do want to play for something you want even more. Consider carefully.

Might of Night ⚡2

Action

+$

Sacrifice: You may discard a card for +5 🔥.

ENG_40_RA_BB

DISCARD EFFECTS

The only thing better than getting a boost for discarding a card is having cards in your hand that give you even more value for discarding them! Darkus is full of cards with potential synergy with discarding—In fact, you may even be able to play the cards you discard for free!

Shadow Coil ⚡3

Action

+4

If this is discarded, you may play it for free.

ENG_46_RA_BB

FORCING DISCARDS

You won't be the only one discarding cards if you play Darkus. Some cards give you the ability to force your opponent to discard as well! You can use this ability to make sure your opponent doesn't get a big card advantage on you thanks to your Sacrifice moves—or you could even get their hand to be smaller than yours!

Cycling Madness ⚡3

◆ Action

You draw a card and your opponent discards a card, return this to the bottom of your deck.

ENG_33_CO_BB

DESTROYING OR STEALING HEROES

Heroes often have powerful passive effects that can give you and your opponent a big leg up. Darkus cards give you greater control over who has which Heroes on their board—you could have the chance to destroy or even take control of one of your opponent's Heroes!

Garganoid's Gaze ⚡2

◆ Action

Destroy a Hero with cost 4⚡ or less.

ENG_37_RA_BB

MIND GAMES

Sometimes Darkus cards give you an extra opportunity to throw your opponent off their game. You may have cards that give your opponent a choice where *neither* outcome is good for them. What will they choose?

Gravity Shift ⚡5

Action

Choose a Bakugan. Your opponent chooses if it gets +1000 or +10 ⚡.

ENG_38_SR_BB

WHAT'S NEW FOR DARKUS IN RESURGENCE

SEARCHING YOUR DECK

The first expansion gives Darkus more tools to make sure the cards they want are in their hand when they want them, by giving you the ability to search your deck for certain types of cards.

Dark Fortune ⚡3

Action

Search your deck for an Evo card, reveal it and put it into your hand. Then shuffle your deck.

ENG_13_SR_BR

REVEALING AND STEALING YOUR OPPONENT'S CARDS

Talk about mind games—the new expansion gives Darkus some very powerful ways to not only see what your opponent has up their sleeve, but to use some of their abilities for yourself. Not only does this put other Factions' abilities in your hands, it also keeps your opponent from being able to play them!

Mind Control ⚡5

◈ Action

Your opponent reveals their hand. You may play an Action card from it for free, gain its effect and put it in your opponent's discard pile.

ENG_19_AR_BR

WHAT'S NEW FOR DARKUS IN AGE OF AURELUS

MAGNUS MADNESS

The new Hero card for Darkus in Age of Aurelus has tons of potential for devastating combos—especially if your deck has three copies!

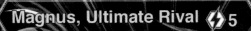

Magnus, Ultimate Rival ⚡5

Hero

When you play this, search your deck for a card. Then shuffle your deck.

If you have three of this in play, your Bakugan get +300 🅱 and +3 🔥.

ENG_69_BE_AA

Maximus Nillious Ultra ⚡ 6

🛡1000 EVO 10 🔥

🛡: +1000 𝐁

If you control Magnus, +20 🔥.

ENG_116_BE_AA

HAOS ABILITIES AND STRATEGIES

If you have a Haos Bakugan on your team, you can put Haos cards in your deck. Haos is all about momentum and control. It wants to collect the most BakuCores and Heroes, then use their abilities to snowball their power.

DOMINATION

The signature move of Haos is Domination. Cards with this ability give you a special boost if you hold more BakuCores than your opponent. So be sure to rack up those BakuCores!

Beaming Blaster ⚡6

Action

+6🔥

Domination - If your Bakugan hold the most BakuCores, +12🔥 instead.

ENG_58_CO_BB

MANIPULATING BAKUCORES

A Haos player benefits from having more BakuCores—and sometimes a Haos player has cards that allow them to get more BakuCores—even ones your Bakugan didn't pick up during a roll!

Consort ⚡3

Action

Attach a BakuCore from the Field to an open Bakugan.

ENG_62_RA_BB

HERO SYNERGY

Having Heroes in play can help you win no matter which Factions you're playing. But a Haos player sometimes gets an even bigger boost from having as many Heroes in play as possible. If you're playing a deck with Hero synergy cards, don't forget to choose some awesome Heroes to go with them!

Revitalize ⚡3

Action

+4🔥 for each Hero you have in play.

ENG_73_SR_BB

DESTROYING EVOS

If your opponent has played a powerful Evo, you may find it harder to win Brawls. Luckily, Haos cards give you lots of ways to take those Evos out of play, spoiling your opponent's plans.

Wane ⚡2

Action

Destroy an Evo that was not played this turn.

ENG_80_RA BB

SCRYING

Scrying means looking into the future! With some Haos cards, you can do just that by looking at your next few cards in your deck. When given the chance to put them back in any order, you can help your game by thinking about which cards you'd like to draw next, which cards you don't mind discarding, and what you think is most likely to happen next in the game.

The Sky's Hymn ⚡1

Action

Look at the top three cards of your deck. Put them on top of your deck in any order.

Domination: If your Bakugan hold the most BakuCores, draw a card.

ENG_78_SR_BB

TAKING HAOS TO THE NEXT LEVEL

With the Resurgence expansion, Haos has even more options for racking up BakuCores, Hero synergy, and controlling the Evos on the board.

Mega Punch ⚡1

Action

Attach a 🔩 from the Field to an open Bakugan.

ENG_33_CO_BR

WHAT'S NEW FOR HAOS IN AGE OF AURELUS

BIG ENERGY MOVES

With Age of Aurelus, Haos gains the ability to sometimes play high-Energy-cost cards for free, especially when you use your Energy wisely!

Haos Suplex ⚡6

Action

+7 ⚡

If you've played a card that costs 5⚡ or more this turn, you may play this for free.

ENG_25_C0_AA

PYRUS ABILITIES AND STRATEGIES

If you have a Pyrus Bakugan on your team, you can put Pyrus cards in your deck. Pyrus is the most aggressive Faction, whose members aim to take out opponents before they even have a chance to get their strategy going. Pyrus wants to end the game quickly and victoriously!

FURY

Fury is the Pyrus signature ability. Many of your Pyrus cards will give you extra effects if your hand is empty after you play them. So you're going to want to play your cards early and be strategic about which card you play last, so that you can reap the benefits of this powerful ability.

Fire Vortex ⚡6

Action

+6 🔥

Fury - If you have no cards in hand, +12 🔥 instead.

ENG_92_CO_BB

SHUFFLING

How to get your hand size down? One method Pyrus offers is cards that let you shuffle cards from your hand back into your deck. You lose the ability to play those cards right away, of course. But in return, you get a higher life total, a better shot at getting your Fury boost, and an extra way of getting your best Flip cards out of your hand and back into your deck. Use wisely!

Cyndeus Stand ⚡2

◈ Action

Shuffle any number of cards from your hand into your deck. +1 🔥 for each card shuffled.

ENG_86_SR_BB

SABOTAGE

As you speed the game up, you want to slow your opponent down. That's why Pyrus has many cards that put a stop to your opponent's plans in the most aggressive way possible—by outright destroying their BakuCores, Heroes, and Energy.

Tip: Destroying BakuCores and Heroes is particularly powerful against Haos opponents. Destroying Energy will be especially helpful when facing Ventus.

Hot Potato ⚡2

Action

Remove an enemy Bakugan's BakuCore and negate its effect. You return the BakuCore onto the field face down.

ENG_95_RA_BB

DAMAGE, DAMAGE, DAMAGE!

When Pyrus cards offer Damage boosts—whether it's as a core effect, DoubleStrike, a Fury effect, or a situational effect—it really packs a punch! Pyrus wants to make sure that when it does damage, it does a lot of damage, so that you can defeat your opponent before you run out of cards! You can even surprise your opponent by winning a Brawl with damage alone.

Meteoric Lance ⚡5

Action

+11 🔥

ENG_103_CO_BB

Might of Cyndeus ⚡2

Action

+1 🔥

This turn, the Victor is decided by highest 🔥 instead of **B**.

ENG_104_RA_BB

WHAT'S NEW FOR PYRUS IN RESURGENCE

FORCING ATTACK

The Resurgence expansion gives Pyrus players even more ways to get that extra damage in, with cards that force a Bakugan to attack anytime, anywhere.

Quickfire ⚡0

Action

Make a ⦿ attack for 1🔥 and you may Reroll your Bakugan.

ENG_44_CO_BR

EXTREME DECK CYCLING

When you go through cards as fast as Pyrus does, you should always make sure you have a way to get the cards you need into your hand. The Age of Aurelus expansion gives you more options for doing just that—and for messing with your opponent's hand and life total while you're at it!

Inferno Cannon

⚡4

Action

All players must discard their entire hand, then draw that many cards.

ENG_33_AR_AA

UNCHARGE

Uncharging your opponent's Energy can have a mighty effect on which cards they're able to play, clearing the path toward your victory!

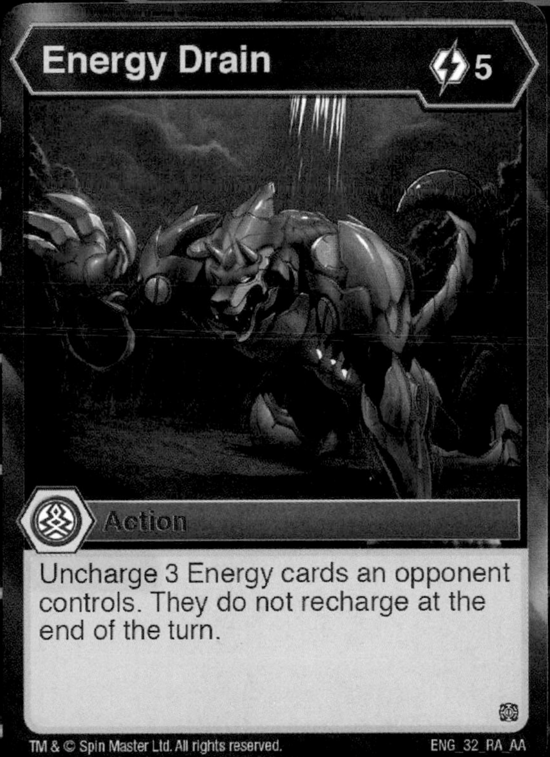

Energy Drain
5
Action
Uncharge 3 Energy cards an opponent controls. They do not recharge at the end of the turn.
TM & © Spin Master Ltd. All rights reserved.
ENG_32_RA_AA

VENTUS ABILITIES AND STRATEGIES

If you have a Ventus Bakugan on your team, you can put Ventus cards into your deck. Ventus is always striving to increase their Energy faster than their opponent. Ventus also likes to slow their opponent way, *way* down.

TURBO

Turbo is the ability that's exclusive to Ventus. These cards give you an extra bonus if you have the most Energy cards in play, so look for every opportunity to Energize—just don't forget that once you Energize a card, you can't play it!

Envenom ⚡3

Action

-5 🌿

Turbo: If you have the most Energy cards in play, draw a card.

ENG_116_RA_BB

ENERGIZING AND RAMPING

Most players only get to Energize a card once per turn—during the Energy Phase. But Ventus has many more chances to add cards to their Energy Zone. This gives you a better chance to gain your Turbo effects, and of course it means you have more Energy to play with next turn, allowing you to play more cards. If you are able to ramp up your Energy a lot faster than your opponent, you might have the chance to pull off some powerful plays much earlier in the game than anyone expects!

Wild Strike ⚡4

Action

-4 ⚡.

Energize this uncharged.

ENG_137_CO_BB

ENERGY, ENERGY, ENERGY!

There's even more Energy synergy in Ventus than Turbo and Energizing effects. You might get a bonus effect for each Energy you have, or for each Energy you use. You might even be able to force your opponent to Energize a card they had been hoping to play.

One with Nature ⚡2

Action

Choose a Hero. Its controller must Energize it.

ENG_122_SR_BB

REDUCING B POWER AND ATTACK POWER

All the Factions have ways to increase their own B Power and Attack Damage, but Ventus has a special talent for messing with their *opponent's* power. You can win a Brawl with a less-powerful Bakugan if your opponent suddenly has less B Power than they thought. And even when you don't win a Brawl, you can stay in the game a lot longer by playing a card that reduces the Attack Power coming at you.

Deafening Roar ⟨⟩ 3

Action

-600 **B**

ENG_114_CO_BB

WHAT'S NEW FOR VENTUS IN RESURGENCE

RECHARGING

In the first expansion, Ventus can get even more control over Energy by gaining the ability to recharge their Energy mid-turn. So not only do you gain Energy faster than your opponent—you can spend it more often as well!

Rabid Attack ⚡4

Action

+4 ⚡

Recharge your Energy cards.

ENG_52_SR_BR

FLIP PUNISHMENT

New for Ventus in Age of Aurelus is the ability to surprise your opponent with benefits for you when *they* play a Flip card.

AtmosFEAR ⚡8

Action

+12 🌀

If your opponent plays a Flip card this turn, you may draw three cards.

ENG_40_AR_AA

WHAT'S NEW FOR VENTUS IN AGE OF AURELUS

AURELUS ABILITIES AND STRATEGIES

For a time, Aurelus was a mysterious Faction, only showing up in Bakugan and their Evos, with no Action, Flip, or Hero cards to add to your deck. That all changes with Age of Aurelus, where this Faction not only has remarkably powerful Bakugan, but also has its own special abilities that give it lots of flexibility and synergy with other Factions.

BATTLE MASTERY

Battle Mastery is the special ability reserved for Aurelus players. Each Battle Mastery card gives you a choice between two abilities. Which one you choose depends on how the game unfolds, but as long as you have a Battle Mastery card in your hand, you have at least two ways to deal with what comes next.

Bodybreaker ⚡2

Action

Battle Mastery: Choose one, +300**B** or +4.

ENG_11_CO_AA

PLAYS WELL WITH OTHERS

If you've played the Bakugan Trading Card Game before the Age of Aurelus expansion, you probably already played with or against teams that paired Aurelus Bakugan with other Factions. That was the only way to play with Aurelus if you wanted to have any cards in your deck! Now Aurelus has its own set of Ability cards that make them even better teammates! Putting Aurelus on teams with other Factions gives you awesome effects in the new cards. This can give you amazing synergy with your Aurelus Power cards from other Factions, too.

Avalanche ⚡2

▶ Action

+200 **B**

If you have played a card from three different factions this turn, +800 **B** instead.

ENG_10_RA_AA

VERY POWERFUL BAKUGAN

Even before the Age of Aurelus expansion, Aurelus was known for having very powerful Bakugan, especially in terms of B Power. Adding one to your team can beef up your strength, no matter which other Factions are your favorites!

Garganoid Ultra

B700

3

🦇: +400**B**

ENG_301_CC_BB

FLIP CARD STRATEGIES

Flip cards can only be played when you turn them over during a Damage Phase after losing a Brawl. If you still have enough Energy left, you can pay the cost and play the card. This could help you get out of taking any more damage, or give you other benefits. Choose carefully which Flip cards to include in your deck—they might just save your game when you least expect it!

STOPPING DAMAGE

The core function of a Flip card is to stop damage. Every Faction has some cards that do this, usually by stopping damage from a certain Faction or by stopping damage from all Bakugan that are NOT part of a certain Faction. You'll probably want to include at least a few of these in your deck, in order to give yourself a good chance to stop damage when it starts coming your way.

Vacuum

⚡0

Flip

ENG_55_CO_AA

Starting with the Resurgence expansion, you'll also find Flip cards that do the same thing with specific types of BakuCores.

Fierce Charge ⚡3

Flip

⬡ non-⬡

ENG_54_CO_AA

Confuse ⚡1

Flip

⬡ a Bakugan holding 🦇 or 🔱.

ENG_67_CO_BR

MORE FACTION ABILITIES

Sometimes, Flip cards are another way that a given Faction's signature abilities come into play. You can't usually control when you'll get the chance to play these abilities the way you would if they were Action cards in your hand—they flip over when they flip over!—but they still offer you a chance to gain some ground, even while you're taking damage.

Photosynthesis ⚡2

Flip

Energize this uncharged.

Shadow Breath ⚡4

Flip

Take control of a Hero.

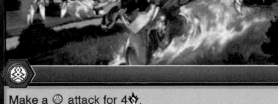

Spontaneous Combustion ⚡4

Make a ⊙ attack for 4🔥.

SPECIAL POWERS

Other times, a Flip card that comes into play gives you the chance to play an ability you would never be able to play from your hand. These unique cards can add an element of surprise and fun to your Damage Phase—surprise for your opponent, fun for you!

Blackhole ⚡3

Flip

End the turn. Nothing else can happen this turn, start the next turn. (Cards cannot be played, remaining damage vanishes and Energy Cards do not recharge.)

Brain Geyser ⚡4

Flip

Draw all remaining damage from this attack. (Instead of flipping the cards into your discard pile your hand.)

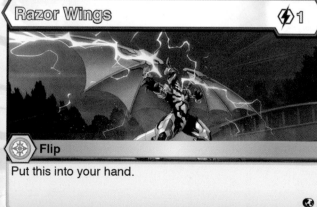

Razor Wings ⚡1

Flip

Put this into your hand.

EVO CARD STRATEGIES

Evo cards make your starting Bakugan even more powerful, usually by giving them higher B Power and Attack Damage. They can also offer you lots of special abilities that can help you tailor your strategy and win!

BIG, BIGGER, BIGGEST!

Evos range from Hyper to Titan to Maximus! Each one is bigger and stronger than the last. You can include any and all tiers of Evos in your deck—just make sure the character name and Faction matches one of the Bakugan on your team!

Fangzor

B600

1

Fangzor

B700

2

🛡: +5

Fangzor

B400

1

🌀: +1 and

BONUSES

In addition to having a higher B Power and Attack Damage themselves, your Evo might give you extra power when used with certain BakuCore types.

Hyper Pegatrix

⚡ 4

B 900 | Evo | 3 🔥

🛡: +400 **B** and +8 🔥

VICTORS AND UNDERDOGS

Your Evos might also offer you extra boosts if you are the winner of a Brawl—or even if you're not! Look out for Victor or Underdog text on your cards.

Hyper Cubbo ⚡2

B400 · Evo · 8 🔥

Underdog: When this opens, if it has lower **B** than the opposing Bakugan, your opponent must discard a card.

ENG_106_RA_AA

Hyper Hydorous Ultra ⚡3

B700 · Evo · 5 🔥

Victor: You may play an ⬤ card with cost 4⚡ or less for free.

ENG_222_AR_RR

MORE POWER!

Sometimes your Evos offer extra abilities are so powerful that they blow your Action cards—and more importantly, your opponent's—out of the water.

Titan Pandoxx Ultra ⚡4

B800   Evo   3 ⬥

Treat all BakuCores attached to your other Bakugan as though they are attached to this.

TM & © Spin Master Ltd. All rights reserved.   ENG_130_AR_AA

Titan Trox Ultra ⚡5

B1000   Evo   10 ⬥

Victor: You may Energize any number of cards in your hand uncharged.

If you control Wynton Styles this gets +1000**B** and +10⬥.

Titan Nobilious Ultra ⚡6

B700   Evo   6 ⬥

When you play this, both players must destroy all but three Energy cards they have.

TM & © Spin Master Ltd. All rights reserved.   ENG_101_AR_AA

HERO CARD STRATEGIES

After you play a Hero card, it stays on the board until someone takes it out somehow. This means that its powers could still be in effect long after you play it, giving you ultimate value for your Energy.

POWER BOOSTS

Sometimes a game just comes down to who has the most B Power and Attack Damage. And sometimes a Hero card can help you get there—but instead of boosting your power only when you play it, a Hero card boosts *all* your Bakugan.

Shargo Ronin ⚡1

Hero

When you open a Bakugan, it gets +100**B**.

Lightning ⚡2

Hero

Your Bakugan get +100**B** and +1⚡.

ENGINES

A Hero card that sticks to the board could give you an ongoing source of card draw or Energy when you really need it most.

Shun Kazami ⚡3

Hero

When you open a Bakugan, you may draw a card.

ENG_77_SR_BR

Dan Kouzo ⚡5

All Energy cards make 2⚡ instead of 1⚡.

ENG_74_BE_AA

LIKE NO OTHER

While you may see the same or similar abilities across different Action, Flip, and Evo cards, many of the ongoing powers Heroes offer are truly unique. Pair them with the right deck and you might be unstoppable!

BEE ⚡1

Hero

When you select a Bakugan to roll, you may turn a BakuCore on the field face up.

ENG_187_SR_BB

Wynton Styles ⚡4

Hero

When you open a Bakugan, you may Energize the top card of your deck.

If you have 15 or more Energy cards in play, your Bakugan have +1500 **B**.

ENG_215_BE_BB

Magnus, Living Arm of Tiko ⚡3

Hero

When you play a card with *Battle Mastery*, you may choose both.

ENG_68_RA_AA

Lia Venegas ⚡10

Hero

When you play this, search your deck for a Hero card and reveal it, then put it into your hand. Shuffle your deck.

+10 🔥 to your attacks, if you control five or more Hero cards in play.

ENG_202_BE_BB

STRATEGY TOPICS

Now that you've studied each Faction's abilities and built your ultimate deck, let's talk about some strategies that will help you play, no matter which Bakugan you have on your team!

FINDING THE PERFECT TIME TO PLAY A CARD

You can play almost any card at almost any point in the game. When do you know when the time is right? Here are some questions to ask yourself before you make a play:

Do you have enough Energy to play your card? Will you have enough Energy left over this turn to defend yourself if you need to?

How many cards does your opponent have in their hand? How much charged Energy do they have on the board? How likely are they to have a counter to your play ready?

Does the card have any situational effects that you can take advantage of right now? Later?

Is the core effect of the card awesome enough to play it now no matter what happens later? (Many times the answer is yes!)

CONSERVING AND SPENDING ENERGY

Energy is a precious resource. Use it wisely, and don't waste it.

Using Energy to boost your Bakugan's B Power early in a turn could help you win that Brawl. If you do win, you won't be sorry to have spent that Energy. But if you don't win, you don't get to recharge that Energy until your next turn, after you've taken the Attack Damage from your opponent's Bakugan. If you flip over a good Flip card, you might not have enough Energy left to use it to stop damage.

So how do you know when it's worth it? You have to use your best judgment. Keep an eye on how many cards and how much Energy your opponent has left. If they are almost out of steam, they're less likely to be able to surprise you with a play of their own.

WHEN NOT TO ENERGIZE

If you need all the cards in your hand, you may decide it's more important to have those options available than to have one more Energy—that's your decision to weigh. Chances are, you'll want to Energize a card every chance you get early in the game. But later on, you'll have more flexibility to decide if you have enough Energy and would rather have the cards in your hand.

If you're near an end of a turn and you have a lot of Energy left, you may want to play a card even if you can't use its effect right away—perhaps getting a Hero or Evo out on the board now will come in handy later, and starting at the beginning of next turn, you'll still have that character on the board and all your Energy recharged!

ANTICIPATING YOUR OPPONENT'S PLAYS

No matter which Factions you play and which strategies you like best, it always helps your game to know as much about *all* the Factions as you can. Why? Because then you'll know what kinds of strategies and abilities your opponent is most likely to use.

For instance, you might be more careful when you play your Heroes if you're playing against Haos or Darkus, because you know they're likely to have options to remove them.

If you're playing against Pyrus, you might be more likely to use your Energy and cards stopping attacks early in the game than with other Factions, because you know they're the most aggressive Faction.

The more you play, the more you learn! Pay close attention to what your opponent does and which cards and Bakugan they choose to use. It might just help you make a decision in a future game!

AGGRO VS. CONTROL

Most decks fall somewhere on the spectrum between "aggressive" and "control."

Players using aggressive decks want to do as much damage as possible, as quickly as possible.. They want to end the game fast because they focus most of their strategy into getting damage in early. If the game goes too long, aggressive decks often run out of steam and will be vulnerable to their opponent's late game plays, because the deck was built with a shorter game in mind.

One aggressive strategy is to go for the highest B Power possible, shutting opponents out from ever winning a Brawl in the first place. Another is to make sure the Attack Damage itself is highest, so that each attack packs a big punch! Whichever tactic players with aggressive decks take (or if they use both!), having cards with low Energy costs is key: They're planning to make all their big plays early in the game before either player has Energized very many cards.

Players using control decks play more defensively, trying to outlast their

opponent and stop them from using their strategies and attacks. At first it may seem like a control deck isn't getting anywhere—simply slowing their opponent's attacks without making many of their own. But if control players can use their deck's defenses to survive until the later game, they can turn the tables just when their opponent is out of options.

You will probably find more Flip cards in a control deck than an aggressive deck, because players who use aggressive decks plan on doing most of the attacking, while players who use control decks have incentive to just stay alive and stop attacks. Control decks might also have a lot more cards that simply negate their opponent's actions or destroy their Heroes or Evos, as opposed to adding B Power or Attack Damage. Meanwhile, for players with control decks, there may be an advantage to hitting opponents for smaller Attack Damage at a time—that way, they're more likely to waste Flip cards on very little damage, or not use them at all.

Which way do you like to play? Build your deck to make it the most fun for you!

OPENING PACKS

So now that you know all about the awesome abilities and characters you can add to your deck, where do you find the cards? By opening packs! Each pack has ten cards, including at least one that has a shiny Hex foil coating!

There are five rarity levels of Bakugan cards—the rarer they are, the harder they are to find!

- Common

- Rare

- Super Rare

- Awesome Rare

- Bakugan Elite

The cards you find in booster packs are the cards you use to customize your decks. You might find any Faction, any card type—any card!—in a pack. If you open a card you don't plan to use right now, you could trade it to a friend for a card you need, or save it in case you want to try a different deck in the future!

SYMBOL GLOSSARY

Your cards and BakuCores might have any of these symbols. Refer here when you need a refresher on what each one means!

 B Power, or the score used to determine which Bakugan wins a Brawl.

 Attack Damage, or how many cards the Victor causes their opponent to turn over from their deck after winning a Brawl.

 DoubleStrike. Bakugan with DoubleStrike deal twice their Attack Damage when attacking.

 ShadowStrike. Bakugan with ShadowStrike can't have their B Power or Attack Damage reduced.

 FrostStrike. Flip cards cost 1 additional Energy for each point of FrostStrike the attacking Bakugan has.

 Energy, or the cost of playing a card. Pay the indicated amount of Energy by uncharging Energy cards you control.

Aquos Faction

Aurelus Faction

 Darkus Faction

 Haos Faction

Pyrus Faction

Ventus Faction

Stop Attack Damage. When followed by a Faction symbol, stop Attack Damage being dealt by Bakugan of that particular Faction. Usually seen on Flip cards.

 Fist BakuCore. Primarily modifies Attack Damage.

 Flaming Fist BakuCore. Primarily modifies Attack Damage at higher values, and includes some other actions.

 Shield BakuCore. Primarily modifies B Power.

 Magic Shield BakuCore. Primarily modifies B Power at higher values and also includes some other actions.

 Helix BakuCore. Often has traps, combat keywords, and modified B Power and Attack Damage.

Now that you know all the secrets of an expert Brawler, let's get out there and Brawl! See you on the Hide Matrix!